# The Magic Gifts

## A folk tale from Korea

Retold by Russell Punter
Illustrated by Gabo León Bernstein

Reading consultant: Alison Kelly
Roehampton University

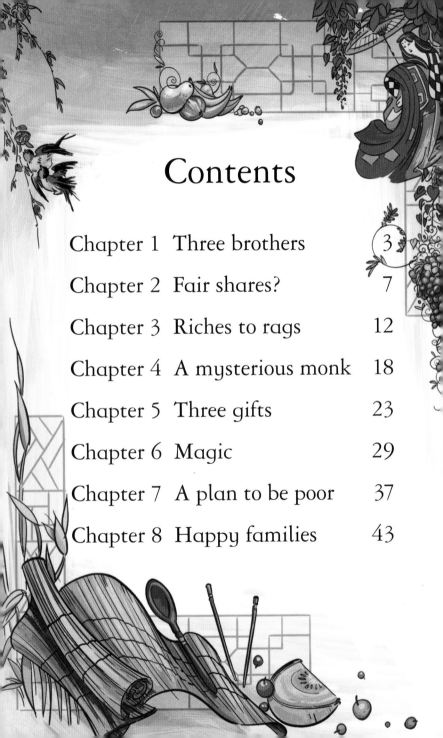

# Contents

Chapter 1  Three brothers    3

Chapter 2  Fair shares?    7

Chapter 3  Riches to rags    12

Chapter 4  A mysterious monk    18

Chapter 5  Three gifts    23

Chapter 6  Magic    29

Chapter 7  A plan to be poor    37

Chapter 8  Happy families    43

# Chapter 1

# Three brothers

Long ago, a man called
Chang lived with his three
sons – Yong, Chin and Ying.

3

Chang was very old and very rich. One day, he called his sons to his bedside.

"I want you to make me a promise," he croaked.

"When I die, I want you to share my fortune equally. You must live together happily."

Chin was glad to agree. But his older brothers didn't sound so happy.

# Chapter 2

# Fair shares?

Not long after, Chang died
and the brothers shared out
his fortune.

"I'm the oldest," said Yong, grandly. "I should have the largest share."

"I'm nearly as old as you," whined Ying. "I deserve a large share too."

So Yong and Ying each took a big share of the fortune. "The rest is yours," they told Chin.

Chin was left with a tiny bag of silver coins.

"Thank you," said Chin. Unlike his greedy brothers, he didn't care for money.

We're rich!

Ha, ha!

Ying and Yong couldn't wait to spend their cash. Soon the house was full of new furniture.

"There's no room for you, Chin," said Ying. "You'll have to move out."

So Chin bought an old hut in the village. His home was simple but he was happy.

# Chapter 3

# Riches to rags

Chin spent his days with the poor villagers. He used his money to help them.

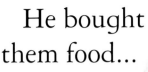

new
clothes...

and even paid
their rent.

He never spent a penny
on himself.

13

Meanwhile, Chin's brothers used their share of the fortune to make even more money.

They bought a huge house...

silk clothes...

and sparkling jewels.

They spent every single penny on themselves.

One day, Ying and Yong
saw a man dressed in rags. He
looked familiar.

It was Chin. He had given
away all his money and was
the poorest man in the village.

"You can't go around like that," said Yong.

"You're making our family look bad," added Ying.

"Leave the village right now," said Yong. "And don't come back until you're rich."

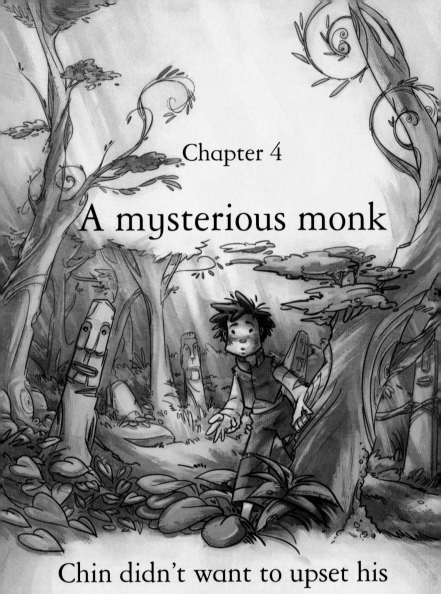

# Chapter 4

# A mysterious monk

Chin didn't want to upset his
brothers, so he left the village.
He walked for miles and miles.

At last, he came to a wide stream. He took off his shoes and dangled his tired feet in the cool water.

"Excuse me," said a voice. Chin jumped. Behind him stood an old monk.

"I'm on my way back to my temple," said the monk. "But I can't get across the stream."

The bridge has broken.

Chin was tired, but he was happy to help. "No problem," he said. "Jump on my back."

The old man held on tightly.
Chin carefully waded through
the rushing water.

The monk and his bundle
were heavier than they looked.
But Chin kept going.

When Chin reached the
other side of the stream, the
monk gave a weak sigh.

"Could you carry me back to
my temple?" he asked.

"No problem," puffed Chin.

# Chapter 5

# Three gifts

After a long walk, Chin and the monk arrived at a lonely, deserted temple.

"Where are the others?" asked Chin.

"I'm the only one here," said the monk. "It's a hard life."

Chin felt sorry for him. "I'll stay and help you," he said.

24

Chin spent the next few months sweeping floors...

mending things...

and copying out books.

One day, the monk noticed Chin looking sad. "What's the matter?" he asked.

"I miss my brothers and the villagers," sighed Chin.

"Then you must return,"
said the monk. "I'll be alright
on my own."

The next day, Chin got
ready to leave.

"I have three gifts for you,"
said the monk.

The monk handed Chin
an old straw mat, a wooden
spoon and a pair of chopsticks.

"They might come in
useful," said the monk, with
a smile.

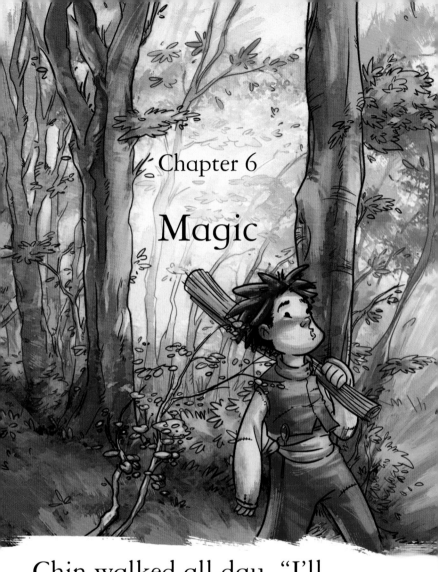

# Chapter 6

# Magic

Chin walked all day. "I'll
spend the night in this forest,"
he thought.

He spread out the straw mat
and lay down on top. It was
thin and worn, but Chin soon
fell asleep.

When Chin woke up, he
couldn't believe his eyes.

The forest had disappeared and he was lying in a big bed in a beautiful room.

Chin poked his head out of the window. He was in the tower of a grand castle.

Chin saw the old straw mat
under the mattress of the bed.

How odd.

Chin picked up the spoon.
It made him think of food. "I
wish I had something to eat,"
he sighed.

Fruit came pouring out of
the spoon. Grapes, cherries,
plums, peaches and pineapples
piled up on the floor.

As he munched the fruit,
Chin looked down at his
torn clothes.

"I wish my suit was as fine
as this castle," said Chin,
taking a spoonful of cherries.

Chin suddenly found he was dressed in silk robes. "The mat and spoon must be magic," he thought.

"I wonder if the chopsticks are magical too," thought Chin, tapping them together.

Suddenly, four beautiful maids appeared. They sang and danced for Chin.

"If only my brothers could see me now," thought Chin.

# Chapter 7

# A plan to be poor

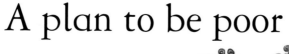

That very day, Ying and Yong
passed Chin's castle.

"I've never seen this place before," said Ying.

"It's enormous," cried Yong. "The owner must be even richer than us."

The two nosy brothers
sneaked inside. When they
saw Chin, they were amazed.

Chin told them all about
the monk and the magic gifts.
Ying and Yong were jealous.

"Maybe if we were poor, the monk would give us magic gifts," Ying whispered to Yong.

"I'm sure he would," said Yong. "Let's get started."

When they got home, the two brothers gave away their sparkling jewels...

new furniture...

and silk clothes.

They even gave away their huge house.

All they had left were the clothes they stood up in.

"Let's visit the monk and collect our gifts," said Ying.

Soon we'll be super, super rich!

# Chapter 8

# Happy families

When the brothers arrived at
the temple, there was no sign
of the monk.

They waited all day. But the old man never appeared.

"Let's stay a little longer," said Ying.

They waited and waited. The days turned into a week.

The weeks turned into a month.

And the months turned into a year.

But the monk never returned.

Finally, the brothers gave up. They trudged back to the village, tired and penniless.

Chin saw them from the window of his castle. "Come inside," he called.

Chin welcomed Ying and Yong into his home and shared his fortune with them.

At last, the three brothers lived happily together – just as their father had wanted.

The Magic Gifts is based on an old
Korean folk tale.

Series editor: Lesley Sims

First published in 2009 by Usborne Publishing Ltd., Usborne House,
83-85 Saffron Hill, London EC1N 8RT, England. www.usborne.com
Copyright © 2009 Usborne Publishing Ltd.

48